the love of
tiger flower

the love of tiger flower

a tale by
ROBERT VAVRA

around paintings by
FLEUR COWLES

with a preface by
PRINCESS GRACE OF MONACO

WILLIAM MORROW & COMPANY, INC.
New York

Library of Congress Cataloging in Publication Data
Vavra, Robert.
    The love of Tiger Flower.

    1. Tigers—Fiction. 2. Flowers—Fiction.
I. Cowles, Fleur. II. Title.
PS3572.A96L6   [Fic]   80-20301
ISBN 0-688-03737-2

Printed in the United States of America
First Edition

1 2 3 4 5 6 7 8 9 10
Book Design by John Fulton

Once again, Fleur Cowles and Robert Vavra capture our imaginations and enclose us in a private special kingdom, offering a glimpse of the beauties and mysteries of love.

Love can open eyes as well as windows and doors that have kept away light and hope. Love lifts barriers that have shut out understanding and compassion. Love enables us to see over the mountains and beyond the horizon and into the heart of the one we cherish.

Just as roses have thorns as sharp as claws, tigers have sentiments as soft as flowers. This charming book will lull you into its fantasies in a most beguiling way.

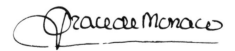

Monaco 1980

"Tiger Flower,
King of the Grass,"
called the
white poppy.
"Come tickle
my leaves
with your whiskers
and
purrrrrrrrr
my petals
into ecstasy."

"Ahhhhhhh,"
sighed Tiger Flower

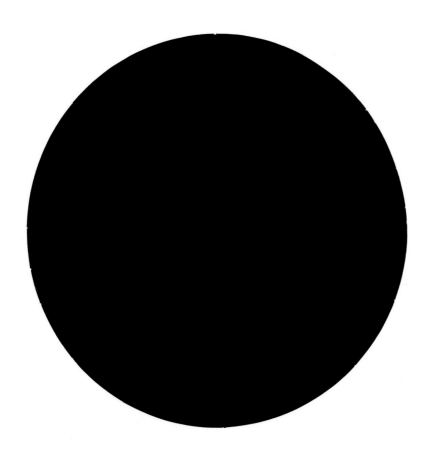

as he caressed
the snowy blossom.
"Poppy,
no female feline
of ebony and gold
could make my
stripes
ripple so."

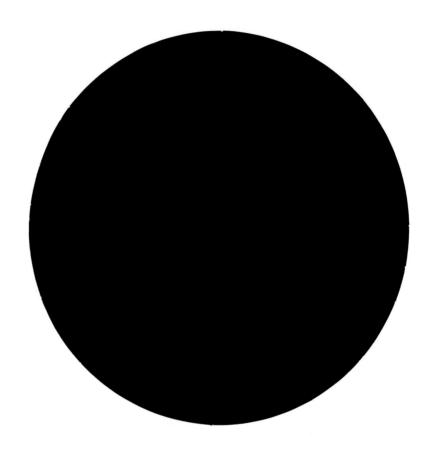

"What kind
of love
is that?"
teased
the creatures
of the grass.
"A cat
and
a flower?"

"Flowers give
us
perfume
and beauty,
asking nothing
in return,"
rumbled back
their
tiny tiger king.
"With light and color
they fill
the dark
dwellings
of our souls."

"But love means
nests and eggs
and raising
young,"
chirped the birds.
"Remember,
there have always
been
tiger families.
No white poppy
will give you
cubs,
or the tall,
tall grass
another king."

"Love means
two—and two
alike,"
chorused
the butterflies.
"Without two
of us

there would
never be
silky cocoons
and the grass
would see
no more
silvery wings."

FLEUR · 78

"Nonsense!"
growled
Tiger Flower.
"I have my
Poppy.
She's the
white tigress
of my dreams.
Besides,
what other
love
will come
to me?"

"*Sitting
and dreaming
among
those blossoms,
a tiger love
it'll never be,*"
answered the cheetah.
"*Now shake
off
that pollen
and follow
me!*

Love is
an adventure,
a voyage—
a search
for the island
of your dreams.
Here,
take my boat
and
cruise
that
exotic
sea."

And as he
set sail,
Tiger Flower
thought,
"Without
Poppy
life's going
to be as
empty
as a shell
on the
sand."

Far out at sea
he met
a jaguar
and asked,
"What,
friend,
are you doing
here?"

"I'm searching for
love,"
answered
the tired cat.
"She's the unknown

goddess of a
sinking
        isle."

"I had a love,"
mourned
Tiger Flower.
"But she's a
poppy,
so I left her
in search of
a female that
looks like
me."

"Flower or not,"
said the jaguar,
"love is love.
Remember,
today you're
little more than
a cub

but tomorrow
you'll be as
old and shaggy
as an antique
rug.
Don't waste
your years
like me,
looking for
an island
in an islandless
sea."

Later,
Tiger Flower
saw,
white and black
and beautiful,
what looked
like his Poppy
gliding
in the deep.
"It must be her,"
he thought.
"She's missing
me."

It was then
the jaguar
again appeared,
this time floating
high.
And as he passed
he shouted,

FLEUR - 69

*"Trust your
heart
and not your eyes.
Who knows,
you might be
a flower
in disguise."*

Once on land
Tiger Flower
was shaken to
the ground.
"Flea!
Flower!
Or feline!"
thundered
the lion-voiced rose
before him.
"That's not what
counts.
Look at me!
Now a flower . . .

now a
cat like you.
To love and be loved
will make you
what you want
to be.

Those scarlet blossoms
adore the jaguar,
but to him they're
only
stems and stamens.
The puma's

enamored
of ivory petals
who aren't aware
that he
exists.
One-way love
keeps two
from ever being
one.

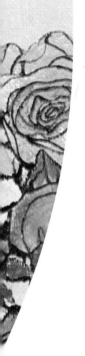

Somewhere,
tiger,

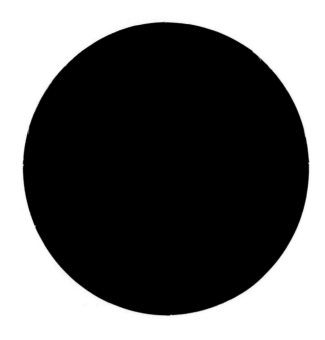

there's a world
of blossoms
spinning through
the universe.
And stalking
that amorous globe
of color and fragrance
is your
black and white
jungle queen."

"It must be
my Poppy!"
answered Tiger Flower.
"She really is
missing me.

But I'm no
scarlet-leaved
passion plant.
I haven't
petals or pollen.
I'm as much
like a flower
as a
winter tree."

"Silly!"
roared the lion,
now again
a rose.
"You love your
Poppy and she
loves you.
One and one

make two
which makes
O N E;
don't you see?
Now let
desire's river
lead the way."

At the water's edge
Tiger Flower's
reflection stared
back at him.
And instead
of fur,
petals and leaves
framed his head.

*It was then
another face
appeared.*

*"Oh, Poppy,"
he sighed.
"At last you're
here,
but honestly
what are we?
Tigers?
Flowers?
Or bumblebees?"*

"Come tickle
me with your
leaves
and I'll

purrrrrrrrrrr
you into
ecstasy,"
whispered
his new-found
jungle queen.

And then
from far
came the jaguar's
voice,
sailing high,
"How wise!
How wise!
They trusted
their hearts
and not
their
        eyes."

OWNERSHIP OF PAINTINGS